Shelly Be[illegible] the Spor[illegible] Queen

Scores a Soccer Goal

By Shelly Boyum-Breen
Illustrated by Marieka Heinlen

DEDICATION: This book belongs to all young sports fans that love to play, work hard, try new things, and dream big. When I was six, I dreamed of playing in the NBA, NHL, NFL and MLB. I worked hard to make my dreams come true, and I made many friends and memories along the way. While I did not end up playing professional sports, I did do a lot of other cool things with my life—like write this book for kids! I am active every day and eager to share my passion for playing sports with others. My hope is that Shelly Bean inspires YOU to play.

ACKNOWLEDGEMENTS: A special thank-you to my youth coaches, parents, brothers, spouse, children, nephews and nieces and many friends who have supported me as I've grown as an athlete and as the creator of Shelly Bean the Sports Queen. Finally, an enormous thanks to the "backers" and Team Bean who worked creatively as a unit to help bring Shelly Bean to life.

For additional copies, visit
www.shellybeanthesportsqueen.com

PUBLISHED BY:
Level Field Press, LLC
2960 Everest Lane
Plymouth, MN 55447
shellybeanthesportsqueen.com

Illustrated By: Marieka Heinlen
Design & Print Production:
Blue Tricycle, Inc.

Boyum-Breen, Shelly, author.
Shelly Bean the Sports Queen scores a soccer goal / by Shelly Boyum-Breen ; illustrated by Marieka Heinlen.
pages cm
SUMMARY: Shelly Bean learns to score a goal, play goalie and gets free tickets to see the pros play.
Audience: Grade 2.
ISBN 978-1-4951-7568-8

1. Soccer for girls--Juvenile fiction. 2. Team sports--Juvenile fiction. 3. Soccer stories 4. Sports stories. [1. Soccer--Fiction. 2. Sports--Fiction. 3. Team sports--Fiction.] I. Heinlen, Marieka, illustrator. II. Title.

PZ7.B6972Shrs 2015 [E]
QBI15-1639

Team Shelly Bean

Shelly Bean loves to try new sports and she wants you to try new sports too! Let's see what she learns to play today. Then follow the tips at the end of the book and start playing with her!

Spike
co-mascot

Shelly Bean
the sports Queen

Buster
co-mascot

Ben
bigger brother

Matt
big brother

Maya
best buddy

Shelly Bean and the gang were on the hilltop playground outside the world famous soccer stadium. Inside, the U.S. women's soccer team was playing Brazil in a big game.

Wow, do you hear them cheering?
It sounds like we scored a goal!

Just then, a soccer ball sailed over the fence of the stadium.

Cool! Should we play a game?
Let's watch the pros play first.
09

Ben and Maya had played soccer, but Matt and Shelly Bean had not. They couldn't believe how fun it was to watch!

That's called dribbling.

LET'S PLAY!
Remember, no hands allowed.
09

The kids tried dribbling and passing the ball to each other.

Shelly Bean tried to kick a pass to Ben but missed the ball.

Shelly Bean didn't
like missing
the ball
and
falling
down.

Matt prepared to kick a goal past Shelly Bean.

She stopped the ball
from scoring but
landed in the dirt
with a THUD.

It was Shelly Bean's turn. She kicked the ball so hard that she fell down again, laughing.

Suddenly, the stadium roared and fireworks exploded in the sky. POW! POW! The U.S. team had won!

The kids waited outside the stadium to return the ball.

Would you like to come to the game tomorrow with your families?
WOW! Front row tickets!

On the way home, they took turns scoring imaginary goals. WHACK! Shelly Bean's kick rolled right between two bushes.

GOOOOAAAALLL!

The next day, they all went to the big game. It was USA versus Japan. To Shelly Bean's surprise, many of the players fell and got muddy.

IMAGINE...
one day, that could be you!
See, Beaner? Falling down is part of the game. Just get back up and try again!

Shelly Bean imagined herself being on a poster someday. She learned to play soccer and even went to a game at a big stadium!

Proud of herself, she made the soccer charm and glued it on her crown of sports.

Shelly Bean placed the crown on her head, stood tall in front of the mirror and thought, "I wonder what awesome sport I'll learn next?"

Tips for Learning to Kick a Soccer Ball

Practicing is best with a partner but can also be done alone in an open space like your yard or a park. These tips are made for right-handed players. Left-handers should simply reverse feet.

1. While standing in place, practice passing the ball back and forth from your right foot to your left foot.

2. When you have passing to yourself under control, start walking forward while passing the ball between your feet. This is called dribbling.

3. When you can walk easily without looking at the ball, begin jogging and dribbling. Keep your head and eyes up so you don't run into people or things. This will help you see your teammates in a game too.

4. Do you have a friend with you? Practice passing the ball back and forth to each other from 5 steps away. After you have 10 successful passes, take two big steps back and practice passing another 10 successful passes to each other, and so on.

5. With a partner, try jogging side by side and passing the ball to each other. Remember to keep your head and eyes up so you can see where you are going!

Now you've got it!

Continue practicing dribbling the soccer ball every day and soon you will be a great team player!

Glossary

Goal: When a player scores the ball through the goal posts past the goalie. A goal is worth one point.

Goalkeeper or Goalie: The only player that can use their hands. Their job is to stop the ball from being scored by the other team by guarding the goal.

Passing: Sending a ball to another player

Dribbling: The basic skill of advancing the ball with the feet while controlling it.

Forwards: The players on a team who are responsible for most of a team's scoring; they play in front of the rest of their team where they can take most of the shots.

Defenders: The 3 or 4 players on a team whose #1 job is to stop the other team from scoring.

Football: Traditional name for soccer

Match: The correct name for a soccer game.

About the Author

Shelly Boyum-Breen grew up playing sports in her neighborhood with friends, her brothers and on her school teams. She found that the life-long benefits of sports for girls were so important that she needed to write this series and inspire girls across the world to play. Shelly resides in Minnesota with her spouse, has two adult daughters and continues to play sports and be active.

About the Illustrator

After designing books and working as a creative director in publishing, Marieka made the leap to become a children's book illustrator. Now with over 30 picture books in print, she loves creating artwork that engages and educates young readers. Marieka always aims to draw an environment where all children can see themselves, as well as the big wonderful world around them.

More action packed books in this Series:

- Shelly Bean the Sports Queen Skates at the Hockey Rink
- Shelly Bean the Sports Queen Plays a Game of Catch
- Shelly Bean the Sports Queen Plays Basketball

And many more...

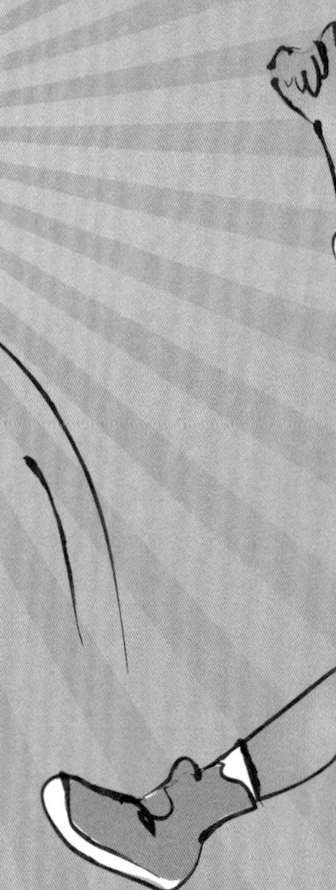